THE CA
THE ANTI
MISSING LUNCH

Written by Vivian Binnamin
Illustrated by Jeffrey S. Nelsen

Silver Press

Library of Congress Cataloging-in-Publication Data

Library of Congress Cataloging-in-Publication Data
Binnamin, Vivian.
    The case of the anteater's missing lunch / by Vivian
Binnamin; pictures by Jeffrey S. Nelsen.
        p.   cm.—(Field trip mysteries)
    Summary: Miss Whimsy's "Fantastic Fifteen" visit the
zoo and discover what happened to the anteater's lunch.
    [1. Zoo animals—Fiction.   2. Mystery and detective
stories.]   I. Nelsen, Jeffrey S., ill.   II. Title.   III. Series:
Binnamin, Vivian. Field trip mysteries.
PZ7.B51183Cas   1989   [e]—dc20   89-24109
CIP   AC
ISBN 0-671-68816-2
ISBN 0-671-68820-0 (pbk.)

Published by Silver Press, a division of
Silver Burdett Press, Inc.,
Simon & Schuster, Inc.,
Prentice Hall Bldg., Englewood Cliffs, NJ 07632.
Printed in the United States of America.

10 9 8 7 6 5 4 3 2 1

Attention All Detectives!

Yes, you can be a detective, too, right along with Miss Whimsy and the Fantastic Fifteen. Just pay close attention to the story and the pictures in the book. There are clues hidden there, and the Fantastic Fifteen will be looking for them. See if you can discover them first!

Our teacher, Miss Whimsy, calls us the Fantastic Fifteen. And for good reason!

Miss Whimsy taught us to peek, poke, and prove. That's right. She solves mysteries. Miss Whimsy is a great detective. Now we're great detectives, too. That is a good thing, because wherever we go, mysteries seem to follow.

"Always check your facts," Miss Whimsy warned. "We're going to the zoo and you never know what mystery lies ahead. You never know how facts may help you peek, poke, and prove."

AMAZING ANIMALS

Speedy Turtles
by Tom P.
If you think all turtles move slowly, you're wrong. Some turtles can swim faster than people.

Giraffes
by Kate L.
Giraffes are quiet. Giraffes are tall. If I had one, I'd name him Paul.

THE OSTRICH
by Kelvin D.
OSTRICHES ARE THE TALLEST BIRDS ALIVE. SOME REACH ALMOST EIGHT FEET.

Lazy Lions
by Casey M.
Lions often spend 20 hours a day resting and sleeping. I don't think I'd like to be a lion.

The Sha
by P.
A shark an amaz. It can sr food mor 1,000 fee

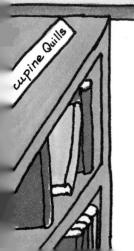

Yesterday we each wrote a report about one animal. Now Dee is a bear expert. Naoto is an elephant expert. Simon is a porcupine expert. And Pam knows all about anteaters.

"Anteaters are the best," bragged Pam.

Our yellow bus drove up to the zoo gate and into a great cloud of dust. People were running around. They were shouting. Animals were rattling their cages and making a ruckus.

"Maybe the elephants have escaped!" said Naoto.
"Maybe someone petted a porcupine!" gasped Simon.
"Maybe this is the beginning of our mystery," said Miss Whimsy.

Mr. Pfeffer, the zookeeper, met us at the gate. He smiled. But his mustache twitched. His eyes darted left and right. And he kept squirming in an itchy way.

"Mr. Pfeffer," said Miss Whimsy, "what's wrong?"

"It started at twelve o'clock on the dot," Mr. Pfeffer said. "At my zoo we feed every animal its favorite foods. Sometimes we go out of our way just a bit. Why, just last week I was off to the Himalayas to find beetles for . . ."

"Yes, yes," said Miss Whimsy, "but what's happening right here? Right now?"

CAMELS

Camels don't store water in their humps. The humps are made of fat which gives them energy for trips in the desert. Sometimes camels really do spit at people.

"Well," began Mr. Pfeffer, "I gave Fred, the anteater, his ants. I gave the bears some honey. And I tossed the camels their favorite grain. They spit at me, too. Right in my eye! Sometimes those camels can be so naughty!"

"So," said Miss Whimsy, "you served lunch. Then what happened?"

We leaned in close. We knew the mystery was unfolding.

Oh, no!
Mr. Pfeffer,
come quick!
Hurry!

DEER
Deer live in many places
on earth. They live in
deserts, prairies, swamps,
woodlands, and even
in the cold Arctic.

"I was about to give the deer their
leaves, and the elephants their branches
and berries," said Mr. Pfeffer. "Then I heard
Phil, my helper, yelling."

"Something's fishy," said Miss Whimsy. "Surely, this is a case for the Fantastic Fifteen."

We thought of the missing ants. We thought of Fred. Fearlessly, we stepped forward.

"Peek!" said Miss Whimsy.

We followed Mr. Pfeffer to the anteater. Fred was hanging by his tail from a tropical tree, looking sad. His foot-long tongue dashed in and out, searching for its missing meal.

ANTEATER
The anteater lives in tropical forests. It uses its strong claws to rip open ant nests. Some anteaters are over six feet long.

"Poke!" said Miss Whimsy, now that we'd peeked at the scene. The Fantastic Fifteen poked around every corner of the zoo. We searched long and hard for clues.

GORILLAS
Gorillas live in African rain forests. When gorillas are excited, they stand on two legs, cup their hands, and slap their chests.

Miss Whimsy blew her whistle and we all hurried back to her.

"We've got it!" cried Simon. "We solved the case of the anteater's missing lunch!"

"Prove it," said Miss Whimsy, proudly.

We pulled out our notes.

"The camels spit in your eye, Mr. Pfeffer. Someone COULD have stolen the ants when you weren't looking," said Pam.

"But," said Simon, "people don't steal ants. Who would want them? And there were no animals loose to take them."

"You had already fed the anteater, the bears, and the camels," added Dee. "You were about to feed the deer and the elephants."

"You keep your animals in A-B-C order, Mr. Pfeffer!" said Naoto, looking at his notes. "Anteater, bear, camel, deer, elephant, fox and right on to zebra!"

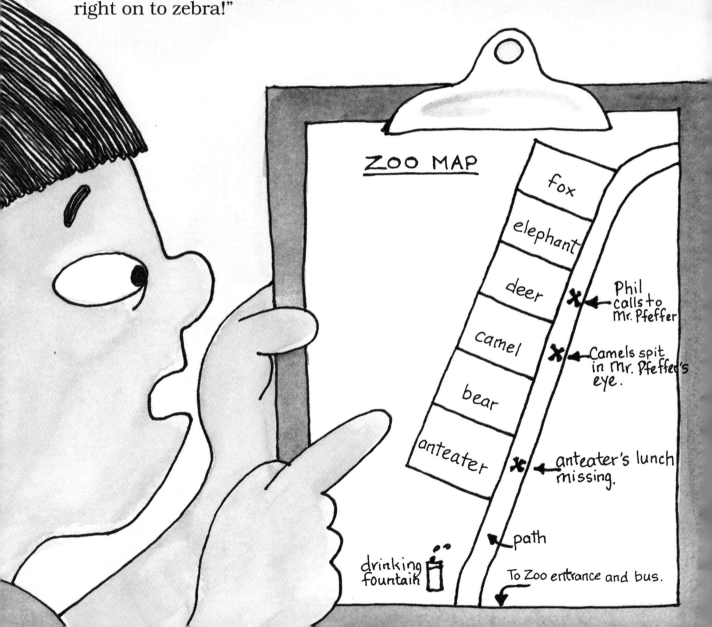

"The bears live next to the anteater!"
said Simon. "The ostrich lives next to the
porcupine, by the way."

"Honey is the bear's favorite food," smiled
Dee, our bear expert. "In fact, they'll rip open
beehives to get it. Their thick fur protects
them from stings."

"And honey is the ant's favorite food, too," said Pam. "No one stole the ants, Mr. Pfeffer. They just went next door for a picnic lunch!"

A quick check at the bear's den proved us right. A team of tiny ants was sharing the honey with the bears. But many of the ants had already wandered off, filled with the sweet honey. There were barely enough ants left for a quick snack, let alone a full lunch for Fred.

"No problem," said Pam, our anteater expert. "Anteaters also like hamburger, milk, and eggs."

"The Fantastic Fifteen are fabulous," said Phil. Then he fed Fred some eggs.

"Thank you, Miss Whimsy," said Mr. Pfeffer. "Your detectives are out of this world!"

"Ah," said Miss Whimsy, "out of this world . . . That gives me an idea for another field trip."
We can hardly wait!

Todos se reunieron en el cuarto, y Pandy agitó el globo de purpurina una última vez.

—Miau-sombroso —dijeron al ver como caía la purpurina como nieve.

¡Escurrigato volvió a la normalidad!

—¡Soy el mismo de antes! —dijo—. ¡Ay, cuánto me extrañé a mí mismo! Gracias, gatos de Gabby.

Entre todos armaron la Casa de Muñecas pieza por pieza, pero Escurrigato seguía con el mismo aspecto.

—Creo que debemos intentar otra cosa —dijo Gabby—. Digamos todos juntos: ¡Agita, agita, agita!

—¡Qué idea tan gatástica! —dijo Bebé Caja; desarmó el globo de purpurina y buscó un plano de la Casa de Muñecas.

—Solo tenemos que armarlo de nuevo —dijo Bebé Caja.

—¡Como un rompecabezas! —dijo Pandy.

Gabby y Pandy dejaron a Pastelillo y salieron en busca de Escurrigato. Escucharon un ruido en el cuarto de las manualidades.

—¿Escurrigato? ¿Qué te pasó?

—Que alguien me ayude —gimió el gato, que ahora era de cartón.

—Hum, quizás si arreglamos el globo, podremos ayudar a Escurrigato —dijo Gabby.

Barrieron las chispas hasta formar una pila. Gabby pellizcó una oreja de la diadema mágica y las paredes de la cocina se cubrieron de galletitas. Todos soplaron a la vez y las chispas volaron hacia las galletas.

—¡Cuántas chispitas! —dijo Pastelillo.

Gabby y Pandy corrieron a la cocina y soplaron las chispas que cubrían a Pastelillo.

—Escurrigato pasó por aquí con un globo de purpurina y luego oí unos ruidos raros —explicó este.

—Ay, no —dijo Gabby—. Escurrigato seguramente encontró el globo con la Casa de Muñecas mezclada y lo agitó. Tenemos que encontrarlo, pero ¡primero te ayudaremos a limpiar!

Pastelillo escuchó unos ruidos raros y la cocina se llenó de chispas brillantes.

—Gabby y Pandy, ¡vengan a ayudarme! —gritó Pastelillo.

—Voy de pasada —dijo Escurrigato entrando en la cocina.

Escurrigato analizó de cerca el globo.

—Creo que está roto —dijo, y lo agitó al salir de la cocina.

Mientras tanto, en la cocina, Pastelillo decoraba unas galletitas.

—¡Chispas, chispas, chispas! —cantaba.

En ese momento, algo brillante llamó la atención de Escurrigato. ¡Era el globo de purpurina con la Casa de Muñecas mezclada! Gabby lo había olvidado allí.

—Oh, el brillo es lo mío —dijo Escurrigato.

Escurrigato se apareció en el cuarto de música, atraído por la tonada de DJ Musicat.

—Hola —dijo DJ Musicat—. Estaba tocando para ayudar a que la bañera regresara al baño. ¡Adiós!

Las burbujas se pegaron a los lados de la bañera. Gabby, Pandy y Gatirena se metieron adentro y las burbujas alzaron la bañera.

—¡Estamos flotando! —dijo Gabby.

—¡PATÁSTICO! —dijo Pandy mientras volaban rumbo al baño.

—Ya sé cómo resolver este problema con ciencia del spa —dijo Gatirena, y se sacó algo del bolsillo—. ¡Usemos mis burbujas de viaje!

Con el permiso de DJ Musicat, Gatirena sopló unas burbujas dentro de la tuba.

Cuando DJ Musicat volvió a tocar, ¡del instrumento salieron burbujas enormes!

—A veces algo de música hace que se me ocurran ideas nuevas —dijo DJ Musicat, y tomó la tuba y se puso a tocar.

—¡Qué tonada tan burbujeante! ¡Me encanta! —dijo Gatirena, ¡y enseguida se le ocurrió una idea!

—Pandy, ¡no te preocupes! ¡Ya hallaremos la manera! Mientras, llevemos la bañera al baño —dijo Gabby.

Entre todos trataron de levantarla, pero era muy pesada.

—Creo que sé lo que pasó —explicó Gabby—. ¡Agité este globo de purpurina y todo se mezcló!

—¡Ay, no! ¿Cómo vamos a arreglarlo? —preguntó Pandy.

DJ Musicat se acercó entonando un tema muy chévere. Se detuvo en cuanto vio la bañera.

—¿Una bañera en el cuarto de música? —dijo—. Qué buena onda.

En el cuarto de música, Gatirena estaba muy molesta.

—¡Menos mal que están aquí! —dijo—. Me iba a dar un baño cuando escuché unos ruidos raros y... ¡puff! ¡De pronto me vi en otro lugar!

—Más vale que entremos y lo arreglemos —le dijo Gabby a Pandy—. ¡Es hora de reducirnos!

Gabby se puso su diadema mágica y entonó su canción especial, la que los reduce para poder entrar a la Casa de Muñecas.

Pero cuando miró la Casa de Muñecas *real* se dio cuenta de que también allí todo estaba patas arriba. Gatirena y la bañera estaban en el cuarto de música.

—Eso no va ahí —dijo Gabby.

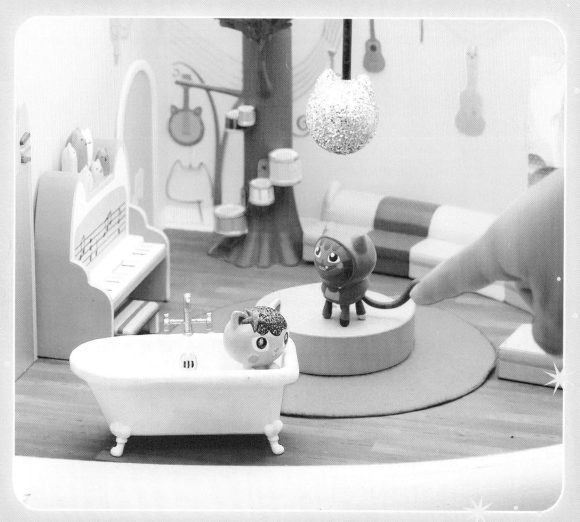

¡Todo en esa Casa de Muñecas estaba fuera de lugar! El techo estaba en el suelo, las orejas, a los lados... y cuando Gabby agitó el globo se oyeron unos ruidos raros.

—Parece que está rota —dijo Gabby.

Gabby sacó una gatástica entrega para la Casa de Muñecas del Buzón Miau Miau. ¡Era un globo de purpurina con la Casa de Muñecas adentro! Pero...